ISBN 1 85854 520 X
© Brimax Books Ltd 1998. All rights reserved.
Published by Brimax Books Ltd, Newmarket,
England, CB8 7AU 1998.
Second printing 1998.
Printed in Spain.

Anna

GROWING UP
ON THE FARM

GILL DAVIES
Illustrated by
STEWART LEES

BRIMAX • NEWMARKET • ENGLAND

BUBBLES

It's lovely blowing bubbles;
To watch them grow is fun.
They are full of rainbow patterns
That shimmer in the sun.

I wish I were a bubble
And I could fly up to the sky,
To see the farm way down below
While I am floating high.

But bubbles burst of course;
They are such shiny, tiny balls.
And when you catch them in your hands
There's nothing there at all.

So I shall sit here with the hens
And blow my breath inside;
So just a little bit of me
Can fly up for a ride.

COUNTING PIGLETS

I try to count the piglets
Mrs Sow had yesterday.
But it's hard, for they keep moving
Or getting in the way.
I think that six are pink
And three have big brown spots;
And certainly nine curly tails
Are wriggling a lot.
Then suddenly another snout
Squiggles into view . . .
That means there are ten piglets
And forty trotters - Phew!

THE KITE

We've climbed to the top of Windy Hill
To fly my brother's kite.
"Run down the grassy slope," says Jack.
"But mind you hang on tight."

The kite is red and yellow
Against a bright blue sky.
It tosses, twirls and billows
And flies up really high.

Then suddenly it makes a dash
And tangles in a tree.
Jack is very angry; he shouts
And shakes his fist at me.

I shall never play with Jack again;
He is shouting at me from the tree.
I've told the cows he's horrid
And they've all agreed with me.

COUSIN HANNAH

"I don't like this farm," said Hannah,
"There are strange smells everywhere.
There is mud inside my smart new shoes,
And the wind has tangled up my hair."

Cousin Hannah did not adore
Our brand new baby calf;
She laughed, "His legs are wobbly,
And he looks like a giraffe."

She said, "My teddy's nicer,
I can hold him how I feel;
Your animals are much too big
And somehow far too real!

It is so much better in the town
There are lots more things to do.
It must be awful living here
As you poor children do."

Inside Mother smiled and said,
"How nice that Hannah's come to stay."
But Jack and I did not reply;
We just wished she'd go away.

KITTEN

Today we found a tiny kitten
Hiding in the barn.
Father said, "Bring her inside,
So she won't come to harm."

We put down some food and milk
In saucers on the floor.
She stepped in them and gulped and sneezed,
Then sat down to wash her paw.

The dog looks like a giant now,
As big as big can be.
He sniffs the kitten, warm and safe,
Asleep upon my knee.

KIDS

There are goats and kids behind the house
And they only mean to play,
But they hit me with their heads
And bounce and bob and run away.

I want to be their friend, but it's hard
When they nudge and bump and bound.
They sometimes topple me over
If I do not stand firm upon the ground.

My brother Jack is like the kids.
He is fun, and says he wants to play,
But then he teases me and rushes around
And bumps and jumps about all day.

DUCKS

I throw the bread into the air
And it scatters on the lake;
Then all the ducks come rushing,
With a quack and splash and shake!
I try to give it fairly,
So every duck has some;
But there's always one who's fastest
And snatches every crumb.

No matter where I throw the bread
Greedyguts is there.
I feel sorry for the smaller duck
Who never gets his share.
A lonely little fellow,
He is fluffy, brown and shy;
When I think of him at night, sometimes
It makes me want to cry.

MRS CLEGG

There are grown-ups who remember
What it feels like when you're small.
And then there are the ones
Who do not recall at all.

Jim who milks the cows
Understands in every way,
He always laughs and talks to us
And thinks of games to play.

But Mrs Clegg who buys the eggs
Sticks her nose up in the air.
Even when we help her find the eggs,
She pretends we are not there.

Mrs Clegg told Jim, "Children
Should be boiled in a stew!"
It is funny to imagine
That she was once a baby too . . .
She might be nice if she remembered
How it felt before she grew.

MY FROG

When Mother and Father are mad at me
Or brother Jack's been mean,
I sometimes go and paddle
And splash all through the stream.

That cheers me up immensely,
And yesterday I saw
A great, big, fat frog watching me
That I was sure I'd met before.

Last year we caught some frog spawn,
All squidgy, slippy, drippy, slop,
We watched it turn to tadpoles
And then to tiny frogs that hop.

I feel certain it was my frog,
The last baby one to go,
Who heard me splashing in the stream
And dropped by to say hello.

PIRATES

I love it when I'm climbing
Right up the apple tree,
So high above the sheep
That they look like toys to me.

I pretend that I'm a pirate
In a ship that tosses to and fro;
I have climbed right up the mast
So the waves are far below.

Then Jack comes out and calls
That it is time to come inside;
He says he sees just where I am
So I need not try to hide.

It is hard to keep pretending
When Jack's tugging at your heel;
I'd make him walk the plank
If my pirate ship was real!

GIRLS AREN'T ALLOWED TO PLAY!

Jack likes riding tractors
While I like ponies best;
Jack always wants to run and chase
When I just want to rest.
But now Jack's brought a school friend
Home with him today;
They've gone off on their own and said,
"Girls aren't allowed to play . . .
Especially not such little ones
For we are grown-up boys."
Then they went across the field,
Making lots of noise.
So I'm sitting on my pony
And I certainly won't cry
I shall dry my eyes, and toss my head
And laugh when they rush by.

DRAGONFLIES

"Let's make a picnic," my mother said.
And then she took ages to cut up the bread.
"Don't hop with impatience," she muttered to me,
"Instead you can help – peanut buttering's free!"

At last, at last, we were outside and running
To the lake where Jack fished and Mother sat sunning.
The lilies were huge, like cups white and gold
With green lily leaf plates, some flat and some rolled.

The dragonflies came, whirring and swooping,
Like small helicopters, shining and looping;
I lay in the grass, wondering, as they flashed by,
Which bit was the dragon and which was the fly?

RABBITS

We had been out for a walk
And were late back home again.
The evening light was golden
All along the leafy lane.

We were tired and slow and quiet
Because the day was at its end.
So the rabbits did not know that we'd
Be coming around the bend.

A car followed us with head lights on,
For the day was fading fast.
The rabbits froze, and stared
Into the beam, like statues cast.

Their eyes were huge and beautiful,
And their fur was rimmed with light
But as the car rushed forward,
They leapt off into the night.

THE BABY

Aunty Ann has had a baby.
She brought her to the farm;
All warm and snuggled in a shawl
And wrapped in Aunty's arm.
When the baby woke, she cried,
Arms thrashing everywhere.
Until we showed the geese to her
Which made her stop and stare.

Then mother held her gently
And rocked her to and fro.
Baby smiled and sighed, then slept
Until it was time to go.
Mother's face looked soft and sad
When the baby left her knee;
So I gave her arm a tug to say
You still have Jack and me.

STRAWBERRY

"We ought to have a donkey!"
My father said one day.
"The children would enjoy it
And I'd love one anyway."
So that is how our Strawberry
Came along to stay.

Strawberry loves the apples
That we pretend to hide.
She has long silky lashes
And eyes that open wide,
And great big ears that listen
To my chatter as we ride.

She seems so much a part
Of our family life each day;
It seems strange we did not miss her
Before she came to stay.

SCARECROW

I dressed up as a scarecrow
For a party yesterday.
Father teased that even 'undressed-up'
I'd scare the birds away!

But our scarecrow who is in the field
Doesn't frighten any crows;
They sit and chat upon his hat
And peck his funny nose.

He is such a cheery fellow,
He does not grumble or complain;
Even when for days on end
He stands alone in pouring rain.

I can see him from my window now,
There is just him, and fields, and sky;
No wonder he is happy
When a friendly crow drops by.

LEAVES

The wind has blown the leaves away
And the trees look cold and bare;
Kitty pounces as the leaves skid up
But I just stand and stare.

Rags is barking very loudly
And chasing around the yard;
He thinks it is exciting
When the wind is blowing hard.

The naked bony branches sway
Against the tossing sky,
The trees have lost their clothing
And they shiver, creak and sigh.

We sweep the leaves to make a bonfire.
Smoke swirls and whirls up high
Where birds are gathering in flocks
To find a warmer place to fly.

MUD

Rags was a naughty dog today,
Though he did not mean to be.
There was mud splashed all over his fur
When he came inside, you see.

Rags ran across the kitchen floor
And straight up all the stairs,
Leaving muddy, dripping bits,
And pawprints everywhere.

Everyone was mad at Rags
Which isn't really fair.
He only came to bark and say
Some visitors were there.

Rags watched me counting pawprints.
There were twenty in the hall;
Then he hung his head and whimpered
So I hugged him, mud and all.

FIRESIDE

Kitty's sitting, I am lying, beside the rocking chair,
Watching pictures in the flames, flicker, curl and flare;
We've been out collecting holly and hung it everywhere,
I can still feel one piece prickling, tangled in my hair.

It's cosy by the fireside to dream of Christmas Day,
What to buy and make, and how to hide my gifts away.
Finding secret places is difficult, you know,
For everywhere I put things, Mother seems to go.

I should be writing cards, not lying in a doze
But I am too snug to move and my eyelids want to close.
Now Kitty's fast asleep, a warm scarf of velvet fur,
She is purring in my ear and I might wake her if I stir.

SNOW

Today the snow came tumbling
In flakes as sweet as lace.
It danced and whirled, white and soft
Like petals on my face.

Jack and I went running,
Scooping armfuls full of snow.
Then we built a great big snowman;
It was fun to watch him grow.

Now the sun is setting,
All pink across the white.
The snowman looks quite lonely
Standing in the fading light.

So I've come outside to talk to him.
I say, "Now don't be sad,
The sheep will keep you company."
And he smiles as if he's glad.